She stepped to the line and took a deep breath. She bounced the ball a couple of times. Another breath. Two more bounces.

Her vision was clearing.

Jackie had spent lots of hours shooting nothing but foul shots. Her dad always told her, "Someday you'll be shooting a foul shot with a game on the line. You can't be thinking you might miss. The shot has to be automatic."

Another long breath and then she hoisted the ball high.

She concentrated on the front of the rim. Then she drove her arm forward and released the ball with a snap of the wrist.

Catch the action with the
Angel Park Hoop Stars!

#1   **Nothing but Net**
#2   **Point Guard**
#3   **Go to the Hoop!**
#4   **On the Line**

POINT GUARD

By Dean Hughes

Illustrated by Dennis Lyall

Bullseye Books • Alfred A. Knopf
New York

A BULLSEYE BOOK PUBLISHED BY ALFRED A. KNOPF, INC.
Text copyright © 1992 by Dean Hughes
Illustrations copyright © 1992 by Dennis Lyall
ANGEL PARK ALL-STARS characters copyright © 1989
by Alfred A. Knopf, Inc.
ANGEL PARK SOCCER STARS characters copyright © 1991
by Alfred A. Knopf, Inc.
ANGEL PARK HOOP STARS characters copyright © 1992
by Alfred A. Knopf, Inc.

Library of Congress Cataloging-in-Publication Data
Hughes, Dean.
Point guard / by Dean Hughes ; illustrated by Dennis Lyall.
p.   cm. — (Angel Park hoop stars ; vol. 2)
Summary: Jackie Willis hopes to convince the coach of the basketball team
in Angel Park that she can play as well as the boys.
ISBN 0-679-83374-9 (pbk.) — ISBN 0-679-93374-3 (lib. bdg.)
[1. Basketball—Fiction.] 2. Sex role—Fiction.] I. Lyall, Dennis,
ill. II. Title. III. Series: Hughes, Dean. Angel Park hoop stars ; vol. 2.
PZ7.H87312Po 1992 [Fic]—dc20 92-6388

First Bullseye Books edition: November 1992

Manufactured in the United States of America

to Andrew Gillis

★1★

On the Bench

Jackie Willis was getting worried.

She didn't like what was happening to her team, the Angel Park Lakers. And there wasn't one thing she could do about it as long as she was sitting on the bench.

"Come on, you guys, watch your passes!" she shouted.

The offense was just not clicking.

Tommy Ramirez, the starting point guard, kept trying to feed the ball to Harlan Sloan, the Lakers' center.

But Tommy had a bad habit.

He would look right at Harlan as he

passed the ball. The San Lorenzo Suns, on defense, knew where the ball was going.

Three times now, the Suns' big center—Manny Rodriguez—had come around Harlan and stolen the pass.

At least the Suns weren't playing well either. The first quarter was almost over, and the score was just 8 to 4 in favor of the Suns.

But then Miles "Tip" Harris, the Lakers' star forward, stole the ball. He took it right out of the hands of a guy named Denny Korman. He quickly tossed the ball to Tommy, and the fast break was on.

Tommy dribbled down the center of the court. Miles took a lane on the outside. It was two on one, and Justin Smagler, a San Lorenzo guard, was running step for step with Tommy.

Miles darted past both players and angled toward the hoop. All he needed was the ball.

But when Tommy tried to make the toss, he lost control. He took an extra step, and the whistle sounded.

The referee rotated his arms around each other and shouted, "That's traveling on number sixteen."

Another opportunity lost.

The Lakers ran back and got ready to play defense.

"I can't believe it," Kenny Sandoval whispered to Jackie. They were sitting next to each other. "There's no way Tommy should be on the first team. A team just *has* to have a good point guard. And you're ten times better than Tommy is."

"Tommy's playing worse all the time," Jackie whispered back. "I think he's trying too hard."

The whistle sounded again.

"You're reaching in, number sixteen," the ref bellowed.

That was the second foul on Tommy already.

"Oh, brother," Stephanie Kadish said. She was sitting on the other side of Jackie. "The guy can't do anything right. But the coach leaves him out there anyway."

Jackie was thinking the same thing.

Tommy was supposed to direct the plays and lead the team. But he just wasn't getting the job done.

Still, she didn't think it was right to say anything. After all, she was the second-team point guard. The other players might think she was jealous of Tommy.

Besides, Jackie didn't want to get the team down on him. That didn't seem right either.

"That's okay, Tommy!" she called. "Let's get tough."

But her best friend, Stephanie, was not so sympathetic. "If the coach doesn't take him out, we're going to lose this game," she said. "The guy's a mess."

Stephanie always said exactly what was on her mind. Jackie wished sometimes that she could be like that herself.

The next time the Lakers got the ball, Miles stayed in the backcourt. When Tommy got in trouble, with Smagler all over him, Miles called for the ball.

Tommy passed to him. Miles broke past Korman and drove toward the hoop. Rodriguez came out to block his way.

Miles kept pushing straight at the big center. At the last second, he bounced a pass to Harlan Sloan. Harlan was all alone. He took the pass and made the easy lay-up.

Jackie could see that Miles had made up his mind to make something happen. Miles was not only a great player, but he *knew* the game—knew what it took to win.

Miles, like Jackie, was black, but he had grown up in Los Angeles. He had played a lot of playground ball, which was where he had learned his great moves. But he had also played on some well-coached teams and knew how to run plays, too.

Jackie had learned most of what she knew from her dad—on her driveway hoop. She had only played one season in a league. She was small and sort of skinny, but she was quick—and *smart*.

Every time she had gotten into a game, she had played better than Tommy. She was sure of it. And yet, here she was—on the bench.

Miles was getting after the Suns on defense, too.

He sneaked in behind Korman and knocked the ball away. Lakers forward Josh Briscoe grabbed it up just as Miles took off. Briscoe led him with a long pass, and Miles had a breakaway.

Miles didn't settle for a simple lay-up. He did a tricky hesitation scoop shot.

"*No!*" Coach Donaldson yelled as the shot went up.

But the ball bounced off the glass and right into the net.

Donaldson still shouted, "Miles, make the sure basket. Lay off that cute stuff."

But Miles was smiling as he ran back down the court.

When the first quarter ended, the score was 10 to 8, the Suns still ahead.

The coach was not happy. "Ramirez, what are you doing?" he barked. "When the defense covers Sloan, find the open man. They're leaving Briscoe all alone. Can't you see that?"

Tommy shrugged.

Jackie felt sorry for him. He was doing his best.

Still, she hoped she would get her chance. She was almost sure she could do better.

"Sandoval, go check in," the coach said.

Kenny got up and pulled off his warm-ups. He waited for a moment. Then he glanced down at Jackie. She could see what he was thinking: "Isn't Jackie going in, too?"

The coach usually put Jackie and Kenny at the guard positions at the same time.

But not today.

Kenny checked in, and Jackie stayed on the bench.

"What's going on?" Stephanie whispered. "The coach has gone *bonkers*, I think."

Jackie didn't know what to think. She glanced around at her parents, in the bleachers behind her. Her dad shook his head, as if to say he also thought the coach was losing his marbles.

Jackie heard the coach say, "Tommy, get out there and *show* me you can do it. I know you can."

But even though things changed, they didn't get any better. Smagler had gone out of the game, and the new guard for the Suns

was not as quick. That should have been
Tommy's chance.

Still, he couldn't make things happen. He
would spot the open player a little late. By
the time he passed, the player was usually
covered.

Luckily, the Suns' tall players were just
waiting for rebounds to come to them. Josh
and Miles were outjumping them and getting some baskets off rebounds.

And on defense, San Lorenzo threw the
ball away as often as the Lakers did.

So the game stayed tight.

Stephanie and Ben Riddle each played for
a couple of minutes, and Kenny played the
whole second quarter.

But Jackie stayed on the bench.

She was starting to think she wouldn't play
at all in the first half.

And then, with just a little more than a
minute to go, the coach sent her in.

Jackie couldn't wait to prove herself.

She took the inbounds pass from Kenny
and blasted up the court. She left her defender standing in his tracks. She dribbled

into the forecourt and hit Harlan with a quick pass.

Then she cut past Harlan, and he dropped the ball right back to her—the give-and-go play.

She was too quick for Rodriguez, who tried to stop her. She slipped by him and laid the ball off the glass for two points.

And she made it look easy.

"Nice move!" Miles yelled to her. He slapped hands with her as the two ran back up the court. The Lakers were still down 24 to 21. But Jackie had suddenly brought some zip to the team.

"Okay, let's get the ball back!" Kenny yelled.

And from the bench, Angel Park's big starter Derek Mahana yelled, "Get after 'em, you guys. Let's get some more before the half."

Jackie glanced at the clock. There were only about thirty seconds left in the half.

The Suns' coach was yelling, "Play for the last shot. Use up the clock."

But that was a mistake. Smagler, who was

now back in the game, tried to dribble across the top of the key. Jackie's hand suddenly flashed out and knocked the ball away.

And just as quickly, she darted past him, picked up the ball, and was gone!

She went all the way for the lay-up, and the Lakers were only down by one point.

Jackie had come in and taken the Lakers' fans by surprise, and they had come to life. They shouted their appreciation to Jackie, and they screamed for more.

Time was running out, and the Suns' coach was yelling for his team to hurry and get the ball up the court for a last shot.

But Sullivan, the Suns' other guard, hurried too quickly to toss the ball in. He didn't expect Jackie to double back.

She darted right in front of Smagler and stole the pass.

And then she fired it to Kenny, who had been covering Sullivan at the base line.

Bam!

Kenny laid the ball in, and the Lakers had taken the lead—25 to 24.

Time ran out before the Suns could throw the ball in again.

The Lakers ran off the court with the lead—and some good momentum.

Jackie was pretty sure she knew who would be playing the second half at point guard.

★2★

Sun Screen

===

"Tommy, did you see what Jackie did out there?" the coach asked.

Tommy nodded and then looked down at the floor. He was a solid boy with dark hair, and he was usually lots of fun. But lately, he looked worried most of the time.

"How does that make you feel? Pretty stupid, huh?"

Jackie wasn't sure what that was supposed to mean. But she didn't like it. There was no reason Tommy needed to feel stupid.

The kids were all sitting down. The coach glared down at them. He crossed his arms and rolled his shoulders forward, so that his neck disappeared into his gray sweats.

"Ramirez, you've got to bring that ball up

the floor with some fire in your eyes. You can't let your defender think you're scared. If Willis can do it, *you* can."

Jackie couldn't believe this. If the coach was so sure *she* could do it, why didn't he just let *her* play?

But the coach was saying, "I want you to go out there in the second half and show me what you can do. Do you understand?"

Tommy nodded.

And that meant he was going back in the game.

Jackie glanced around to see what the others were thinking. Kenny looked at her and gave his head a little shake.

Miles was a lot more obvious. He threw his towel on the floor.

And Stephanie, sitting next to her, gave Jackie a nudge. "That *stinks!*" she whispered.

But no one said anything—out loud.

The coach was now chewing out all the starters. He finished by saying, "Now let's see you kids play like you mean it!"

Jackie went out to the court and took a few shots. Then she strolled over and sat on the bench. She figured she'd be spending her time there anyway. Why bother to warm up?

Why bother . . . period?

Derek came over and told Jackie, "Hey, don't let the coach get you down. The guy wouldn't notice you even if you took a bite out of his big belly." Then he laughed. "Hey, that's not a bad idea either."

Jackie laughed a little, too. But she didn't feel any better.

The worst part was, nothing changed. The Suns took the lead back. And all through the third quarter, the score stayed close.

When Tommy picked up his third foul, Jackie thought she would finally get back in the game.

But no.

The coach had played everyone at least a minute or two. Now he was staying with his starters—except that he left Kenny in for Derek.

Tommy was still struggling to get the ball across the ten-second line. And he was too busy dealing with Smagler to spot the open players and make good passes.

Miles was taking over Tommy's job from his position. He would sometimes yell, "Clear!" The players would move to the left of the lane and let him go one-on-one with Korman.

That worked all right until the Suns switched into a zone. Two players tried to dog Miles most of the time. They could do that because they didn't really worry about Tommy driving into the middle, the way he should be doing.

When the third quarter ended, the Lakers were behind, 36 to 32.

Jackie thought the coach would finally have to give her a chance. But he spent the time chewing on Tommy.

Just when she had given up hope—and just before it was time to go back on the court—he suddenly said, "Okay, Willis, you go in. I guess Ramirez doesn't care whether he plays or not."

That wasn't exactly a vote of confidence. But Jackie was still glad to get another chance. She hurried and got her warmups off.

And it didn't take long to see the difference she made in the game.

She pushed hard up the floor and kept Smagler from setting up in front of her. If he got too tight on her, she would break past him. After she did that a couple of times, he started giving her more room.

She passed off to Harlan a couple of times,

on the high post, and the Lakers ran their plays.

She set good screens, and she spotted the open players. The Lakers were faster, and now that they had some direction and control, they were getting open shots.

Josh hit a short jumper. Then Kenny took a pass off the post and drove the lane for another basket. The Suns had to stop double-teaming Miles.

When they did, Miles started popping the net.

The Lakers scored ten quick points and were suddenly in control.

Then Jackie grabbed a long rebound and dribbled quickly up the floor. She saw that the fast break was covered, so she pulled up and hit Miles on the right side of the key.

He faked his defender in the air and dribbled past him.

When he got cut off, he bounced the ball back to Jackie, who made a hard move to the hoop. She went all the way in for the lay-up.

Big Rodriguez blocked her shot but also slammed into her with his body.

Jackie went flying. She hit the floor hard and then crashed into the mat on the wall.

That didn't stop her, though. She jumped right up.

For a few seconds she saw little flashes of light. But she had heard the whistle and knew she had foul shots coming. She wasn't going to let anyone know that she was a little dazed.

And she sure wasn't going back to the bench.

She stepped to the line and took a deep breath. She bounced the ball a couple of times. Another breath. Two more bounces.

Her vision was clearing.

Jackie had spent lots of hours shooting nothing but foul shots. Her dad always told her, "Someday you'll be shooting a foul shot with a game on the line. You can't be thinking you might miss. The shot has to be automatic."

Another long breath and then she hoisted the ball high.

She concentrated on the front of the rim. Then she drove her arm forward and released the ball with a snap of the wrist.

The ball arched high, with good backspin, and—*pop*—it snapped the strings.

Second shot.

Same motion.

Pop.

Same result.

The score was 42 to 36, and the Lakers were on a roll.

But the Suns weren't ready to give up— not yet. Smagler gunned a long shot that swished through the net from outside the three-point line. Suddenly the lead was cut in half.

The Suns all shouted, but they lost concentration just a second too long.

Jackie grabbed the ball, stepped out of bounds, and tossed it long down the floor. Kenny had darted to the other basket ahead of everyone.

He got two of the three points back— *easy*—and the Lakers hurried back on defense.

The zone was tough, and Smagler couldn't see an opening. He decided to throw up another long bomb, but this time Jackie had a hand in his face.

The shot was an "air ball," and Harlan grabbed it and passed off to Miles. Miles passed to Jackie.

She forced the ball up the floor quickly

and faked a pass. Smagler took the fake and dropped off. Then Jackie went up for a three-point jumper of her own.

When she released it, she was almost sure it was going in. But it hit off the top of the front rim, bounced up to the glass and back to the rim.

Then it rolled all the way around before it . . . *dropped through the net.*

Now the score was 47 to 39.

And Jackie could feel it in her bones—the Lakers were going to run away with this game.

Smagler was beginning to panic. He made a bad pass that Josh intercepted.

Josh passed to Jackie, and she dribbled up the floor. The break wasn't open, so she raised her open hand to signal a clear-out. She passed to Harlan and then took her defender to the left of the key.

Harlan hit Miles, who took the pass, and then stared into his defender's eyes.

He faked left, right, left again. Then *pow,* he broke to the right.

Korman lost him, but Rodriguez tried to clog the middle. He jumped straight up, his arms high in the air. But Miles brought the ball back down and shot an underhanded lay-up beneath those outstretched arms.

Rodriguez brought his hands down too late and only managed to slap Miles on the wrist.

The ball hit the glass and caromed into the net, and the whistle sounded.

The ref motioned that the basket counted. Miles would also get a foul shot.

The score was 49 to 39, and Miles could add one more. Jackie slammed hands with Miles and walked to the key to get ready for the foul shot.

But then she heard the buzzer. The scorer was signaling that a substitution was coming.

She looked around. Tommy was running straight at her. "Jackie, I'm coming in for you," he called to her.

Jackie couldn't believe it.

But she walked off the floor.

The game was almost over now, so it didn't matter that much. But what was the coach trying to say?

The Lakers won, 54 to 45.

Everyone celebrated.

Jackie did, too, but she didn't really feel like it.

★ 3 ★

Spectator Sport

Jackie felt sort of down all weekend. She was glad she had played well—and glad the team had won. She told herself that maybe the coach had put Tommy back in the game at the end only so he wouldn't feel bad.

Maybe she would actually start the next game.

She surely had earned the right.

She just didn't believe it would happen. Still, she didn't *want* to believe what Stephanie was saying.

Stephanie called on Sunday afternoon. "Everyone on the team knows the coach is being unfair," she told Jackie. "Even Tommy knows it. He told me when he was sitting by me on the bench."

"But the coach cares more about winning than anything," Jackie said. "Why would he keep playing Tommy most of the time?"

"Two reasons, I'd say. Number one, he's got a brick for a brain. And two, he doesn't want a girl to be a starter."

"Oh, come on, Steph. Why would he care about that?"

"Okay, then, give me another good reason."

Jackie didn't know what to say. Maybe the coach was seeing something the rest of them couldn't see.

The worst thing was, she knew the coach wasn't stupid—at least not about basketball.

That seemed to leave number two.

"Hey, something good did happen on Saturday, though," Stephanie said.

"What?"

"Those jerky Bulls lost to Santa Rita."

The Bulls were the other team in town—the one that had gotten most of Angel Park's taller players.

"Really?" Jackie said.

"Yup. That puts Blue Springs in first. They've won all their games. The Jazz and the Bulls have each lost one, and we've lost two. So we're not so bad off if we don't lose any more."

"I still think we could win the championship—if we could play the way we did there for a while in the second half."

"Yeah. When you were in the game."

Jackie hadn't meant to suggest that. But she knew it was true.

On Tuesday afternoon the kids practiced in the elementary school gym. Coach Donaldson had the players do their regular drills, and then he had them scrimmage.

He didn't say one word about changing the starting lineup.

Jackie tried not to let her disappointment show. But she played *hard* on defense—and she was guarding Tommy.

The coach was on Tommy's back more than ever. "Ramirez, *think*," he kept screaming. "What did I just tell you?" And then he would demonstrate and have Tommy try again.

But things got worse. And there's no way they couldn't have. Tommy had to be tense with the coach watching every move he made.

When Jackie finally got a turn to play the position, she did a much better job of handling the ball. She was also a better shooter, and she wasn't afraid to drive to the hoop.

Once she dribbled down the lane, and two defenders pulled in to stop her. She hurled the ball to Josh without even looking at him. He banged in a shot off the glass.

"Hey, nice play, Jackie!" Miles yelled to her. "That's what we need to do."

Coach Donaldson didn't say a word.

A couple of minutes later, she took a jumper from the top of the key. The shot was just a little off line.

Coach Donaldson barked, "Don't be gunning up the long shots, Jackie. Be patient. Work the ball in close."

"Coach," Miles said.

"All right, kids, let's—"

"*Coach.*"

Coach Donaldson looked at Miles.

"Teams are starting to play zones on us. And they're clogging up the middle. Shouldn't we try to spread them out with some longer shots? That's what my coach last year had us do."

Jackie felt the sudden silence in the gym. She saw the color come into Coach

Donaldson's cheeks and spread along the side of his neck.

"Well, Harris, I know you think you know everything. But that only works with older players who can put the long shots in. With kids your age, those are low-percentage shots."

Miles's voice suddenly rose. "Hey, Josh and I can hit from outside. So can Jackie. She canned a three-pointer in that last game."

"Yes, she did. But how often is that going to happen?"

"A lot, if you'd let her play. She's one of our best players, and you've got her on the bench."

"That's enough out of you, young man!" Donaldson shouted.

And then silence.

No one moved.

"I'm the coach. And don't forget it."

Miles didn't answer, but he stared straight back at the coach. Everyone else was watching, too.

Jackie thought Coach Donaldson looked less sure of himself than usual.

"If I put someone out there to play," he finally said, "I'm looking at not only his ability, but also his *potential.* A coach has to consider those things."

Jackie tried to think what he meant. Was he saying that Tommy wasn't as good now, but he *could* be better than Jackie?

Coach Donaldson pointed a finger at Miles. "But I don't have to explain my decisions to you. No one tells *me* how to run my team. Do you understand that, Harris?"

"I sure do." Miles smiled. "You mention it all the time."

Coach Donaldson didn't like that at all. "Listen here, young man. Don't you get smart with me, or you'll be the one riding the bench."

Miles didn't say anything. But he was still smiling—just a little.

Coach Donaldson waited a few seconds. He seemed unsure of himself. Finally he said, "All right, let's get back to work. I'll have no more of this smart stuff from *any* of you."

And on Saturday morning, when game time came, Coach Donaldson still had Tommy in the starting lineup.

The game was against the Cactus Hills Clippers—the worst team in the league. Or at least they hadn't won a game so far this season.

But the Clippers did have one *very* good player. He was a kid named Zach Harrison. The guy was fast, and he could really shoot.

Like the Lakers, though, the Clippers didn't have much height. Jackie didn't think they had a lot of talent either.

But when the teams lined up for the tip-off, Jackie saw the problem the Lakers were going to have. Harrison was guarding Tommy.

Tommy was never a *great* player, but he did a lot better when he wasn't pressured. When someone guarded him close—really stayed with him—he got rattled.

It didn't take long for the trouble to show up.

On the jump-off, Harlan got up above the Clippers' center and tipped the ball to Derek. Derek passed to Tommy, and he turned to dribble.

Harrison was right there. He slapped the ball out of Tommy's hands, grabbed it, and dribbled in for a quick, easy hoop.

Kenny groaned. Stephanie said, "Oh, brother. Here we go again."

Jackie just hoped that the coach would give her some playing time a little earlier today.

But Tommy played the whole first quarter.

And things actually went pretty well—because of Miles.

Miles kept coming back to help Tommy. After a while, he was usually the one dribbling the ball across the center line.

In fact, as often as not, Miles would take over from there. He would drive to the hoop and take a shot himself. Or he would pull in defenders and then pass off.

But the Lakers weren't running their plays. And Tommy was hardly involved at all.

On defense, Tommy was having an even worse time. Twice in the first quarter, Harrison slipped past Tommy. Tommy reached back to stop him and got whistled for fouls.

Then, just before the end of the quarter, he picked up his third.

"Okay, get ready," Kenny told Jackie. "He's got to put you in now."

But only a few seconds were left in the quarter, and the coach made no change.

The Clippers threw the ball in from out

of bounds. Harrison took the pass and flashed right by Tommy. He drove down the court and then pulled up and took a three-point jumper.

The ball swished through the net just before the buzzer sounded.

And the Clippers were right back in the game. The score was 13 to 10.

The Lakers all looked disgusted as they walked off the court. The kids on the bench stood up and let the starters sit down. Jackie stood next to the coach—waiting.

But the coach was busy chewing on the starters.

"You're not running the offense!" he yelled at them. "Miles, you're taking the ball and doing anything you want with it. And Tommy, you're just letting him do it."

"Coach, that Harrison kid is all over me. I can hardly—"

"Then go at him. Beat him. You're our *leader*. You've *got* to take control."

The coach left him in the game.

Jackie sat down again.

She glanced around at her dad. He looked mad enough to punch somebody out.

At the moment, Jackie wasn't sure that was such a bad idea.

★ 4 ★

Leading the Way

Miles followed Coach Donaldson's instructions. He didn't come back to help the guards get the ball up the floor.

And Tommy tried to follow instructions, too.

He even played somewhat better. He quit hanging back. He tried to push the ball at Harrison. Sometimes it worked, and he got the ball up the floor all right.

But Harrison adjusted.

One time Harrison swiped the ball out of Tommy's hands and dribbled in for an easy basket. Another time he blocked one of Tommy's passes. The other Clippers guard, a kid named Chase Higdon, picked the ball off.

But Tommy was battling to do his best. He called some plays. And he fed the ball to Harlan on the post—when he could.

When he did get the ball to Harlan, the plays worked pretty well. Josh was getting open. He hit a couple of nice jumpers. When he missed, Miles could outjump the Clippers' rebounders. He got an easy "put back" shot for two points.

The coach put Kenny in the game, and he also got free for a jumper that rolled around and dropped through the hoop.

So the Lakers began to rebuild their lead. With about three minutes left in the half, the Lakers were ahead, 23 to 16.

But then Harrison drove hard on Tommy. Tommy tried to stay in front of him. He banged Harrison with his hip, though, and the ref called a foul.

Number four.

Coach Donaldson called time out immediately, and now Jackie *knew* that she was going in.

But the coach grabbed Tommy by the

shoulders. He spoke nose to nose with him. "You're doing better. Be careful, and don't foul. But don't let up on offense. I'm counting on you."

Tommy nodded.

But then Jackie saw him glance her way and shrug, almost as though he wanted to apologize.

Coach Donaldson put Stephanie in the game for Josh, and Brett Sanders in for Harlan. But he left Jackie on the bench.

The new combination was not a good one.

Stephanie and Brett tried hard, but they weren't confident. Neither one liked to shoot. Miles tried to do what he could again, but the defense was concentrating mainly on him.

A substitute came in for Harrison—a girl named Sandy LeDuc. She wasn't as fast as Zach Harrison, but she worked hard and stayed in Tommy's face.

The offense died.

And LeDuc knew that she could drive on Tommy, who had to be very careful not to foul.

She turned out to be a good shooter. She

drove down the lane for a basket. Then she tried again, got cut off, but passed off to her center. He put the shot in.

Miles came back with a nice little jump hook shot off a rebound, just before the halftime buzzer. But now the score was 27 to 22.

The Lakers couldn't shake this team loose.

Jackie listened to the coach preach to the team at halftime. Tommy needed to do this, and Tommy needed to do that. And finally, "Ramirez, I keep telling you, this team *must* have a leader. Now go out there and show me you can be one."

Jackie saw the coach glance at her, only for a second.

And she saw something strange in his eyes. Maybe he was embarrassed. Maybe sorry. But somehow, she was pretty sure he knew he was doing something not quite fair.

All the same, when the second half started, Tommy was still in the lineup.

And there was no question what the Clippers' coach had told Harrison. Tommy would have to be careful, with four fouls. So go right at him! Either get by him for the basket, or draw that fifth foul.

And that's what Harrison did.

He covered Tommy like a blanket on defense, and on offense, he drove at him *hard*.

And he scored some quick baskets.

Miles kept the Lakers in the game all by himself. The Lakers weren't getting good shots. But when one of them shot—and missed—Miles was in there battling for the rebound.

He got enough points that way to hold the lead. But the Clippers kept edging closer.

And then Harrison faked a drive and pulled up for a jump shot. He missed the shot, and Harlan grabbed the rebound. But Higdon sneaked in and grabbed the ball away from Harlan.

Higdon fired up a quick shot and the game was tied at 34 all.

Jackie could see the game slipping away. And the coach was still trying to make a leader out of Tommy.

This was nuts.

But then it finally happened. With the third quarter winding down, Harrison drove past Tommy. Tommy reached back and caught Harrison across the chest with his arm.

The whistle shrieked.

Fifth foul. Tommy was out of the game.

"All right," Coach Donaldson said, and he sounded disgusted. "Jackie, go ahead and check in."

If the Clippers' coach had known what was coming, he never would have wanted that fifth foul.

Jackie had been sitting on that bench for a long time. Now she had something to prove.

The other players also seemed to come to life. Jackie could feel that they expected good things to start happening.

And good things did happen.

Harrison missed the foul shot, and Harlan grabbed the rebound. He tossed the ball out to Jackie, and she took off so quickly that Harrison was taken by surprise.

Jackie raced to the top of the key, ahead of Harrison. Then she looked straight at Josh and passed to Harlan.

The Clippers' center took the fake and stepped to his right. Harlan rolled the other way and went to the hoop for two.

It was the first time he had scored all day.

Then Jackie got after Harrison. She stayed

right in his face, jabbing at the ball, pestering him.

Harrison looked off balance. He tried to pass to Higdon, but Jackie deflected the ball out of bounds.

Then on the inbounds pass, she stayed so tight on Harrison that he couldn't get the pass. Higdon tried to throw to a forward, but Miles cut the pass off.

Miles passed quickly to Jackie and called out, *"Let's go!"*

Jackie took off like a shot. She was ahead of Harrison, and she kept right on going.

She zipped straight to the basket and went for the lay-up. Harrison tried to block the shot from behind—and he did. But he drew a foul.

Jackie stepped to the line and dropped in both foul shots.

Just like that the score was 38 to 34.

But Jackie knew the Lakers needed a bigger lead.

She didn't cover Harrison close this time. She stayed back and let him bring the ball down the floor. She knew what she wanted to do.

As Harrison crossed the ten-second line,

she came a little closer. She took a couple of deep breaths and acted as though she were tired already.

Just when Harrison relaxed a little and glanced to see where he could pass the ball— *pow*—Jackie jumped forward. She knocked the ball out of Harrison's hands.

The ball flipped high in the air. But Jackie jumped high and caught it. And—still in the air—she spotted Kenny, who had gone after the ball himself.

She hit him with a pass before she even came down. And Kenny had a clear break-away.

Kenny drove the floor and put in the easy lay-up.

Now it was 40 to 34.

And that was the score as the third quarter ended.

Coach Donaldson said, "Okay, nice job," when the team ran off the floor. But he didn't say, "Nice job, Jackie."

He talked about running the plays, about playing tough defense—all the usual stuff. And then he sent the same players back on the floor.

Jackie felt like she had to keep proving herself.

Harrison now knew he had a battle on his hands and he gave Jackie a little more room. That meant she couldn't get by him, but she could make the passes she wanted to make.

And the offense started to click. Jackie had a nice sense of what plays would work. She knew what player was getting open, and she made sure the ball got to that player.

She also made a couple of nice shots herself.

The Lakers won the game going away. The final score was 55 to 42.

When it was over, the whole team congratulated Jackie. Tommy told her, "You did a lot better job than I did. I don't know why the coach won't let you play more."

Miles told her, "Hey, you're the *one*. We gotta have you out there."

And Stephanie told her, "You'll start next game for sure. You watch."

But the coach didn't say so.

In fact, the coach didn't say anything to her at all.

★ 5 ★

Fair Is Fair

Jackie rode home from the game with her parents.

Her dad was angry.

Her mom was furious.

"Didn't he even tell you what a great game you played?" she asked Jackie.

"No. He just told the whole team that we have to start making the offense work. That's the only thing he *ever* says."

Jackie was sitting in the back seat. She was looking out the window as her dad drove through the little downtown area of Angel Park.

It was a warm winter day, even for southern California. The sun was shining bright, but for Jackie, everything seemed pretty dark.

"Kenneth, that isn't fair," Jackie's mom told her husband. "You can see what the coach is going to do. He'll start Tommy Ramirez again next game. Jackie's *earned* that position."

"Hey, you don't have to convince me. Everyone in the gym could see it. Mr. Ramirez even came up to me and said he didn't understand what was going on."

"Well, I'll tell you what I think," Mrs. Willis said. "I think the man doesn't want to admit that the real team leader is a *girl.*"

"Yeah, and a black girl besides."

But Jackie didn't want to believe that race had anything to do with it. "Maybe the coach just doesn't like to admit that he made a mistake when he picked Tommy," she said. "That's the way Coach Donaldson is."

Mr. Willis glanced at Jackie, quickly. "Well, I don't care what his reasons are. He's being unfair. Not just to you, but to the whole team. And I'm going to tell him so."

"No, Dad, don't do that."

"Why not?"

"I don't want to get the position that way. I want to *prove* I deserve it."

"Oh, honey," Mrs. Willis said, "you've already done that. Now I think it's time someone said something."

"No. Please don't. Let me handle it myself—my way."

Jackie saw her dad take a big breath and then let it blow out. "Well, all right. For now. But I'm not going to let this thing go on much longer."

Jackie was relieved. She didn't like the idea of having her "daddy" interfere for her. Still, she wondered what it would take to get the coach to make a fair decision.

That night Stephanie came over.

She and Jackie talked about a lot of things, but the conversation always came back to the basketball team.

"Jackie, I think we could win the championship if the coach would let you play more," Stephanie told her.

"I don't know. I make a lot of mistakes."

"Oh, come on, Jackie. Don't act like you

don't know it. Except for Miles, you're the best player on the team."

"Josh is really good."

"You're just as good as he is—or better."

Jackie was lying in a beanbag chair, with her hands behind her head. She thought about that. She wasn't sure. But she knew she had played well.

Stephanie was sitting on the floor, cross-legged, right in front of Jackie. "Speaking of Miles," she said, "he's pretty cute, don't you think?"

"I didn't know we were still speaking of him," Jackie said. "And anyway, he's about *half* as cute as he *thinks* he is."

"Maybe so. But he *is* cute."

Jackie shrugged, and she tried not to smile.

"Hey, you're blushing. What's going on here? I thought you didn't like him."

"I didn't say that—exactly."

"Ohhhhhhh, Jackie, what *is* this? Are you trying to tell me something?"

"No. I'm not. And I'm not talking about this anymore." Jackie tried to bring the subject back to the team. "The coach said he had to consider *potential*. Maybe he thinks Tommy will be better than me—once he gets some experience."

"No way. Tommy's a klutz. He's still trying to figure out how to get his shoes on the right feet. His mommy probably has to cut up his meat for him."

"Come on, Steph. He tries hard. He—"

"She chews it for him and spits it in his mouth—like a bird."

"Steph, lay off. You're too mean. He's not *that* bad."

"Well, he's not as good as you. And he never will be."

"But the coach wouldn't start Tommy just because he likes him better. Or because he's a boy. That's too rotten. I don't like to think stuff like that actually happens."

"Come on, Jackie, you know it does. Look at some of the stuff kids say to me—because my dad's Arab. Hasn't anyone ever treated you badly because you're black?"

"I don't know. It doesn't seem like it. But

maybe—if they did—I just didn't want to admit it."

"That's being kind of dumb, Jackie. I hate to say it, but it is."

"Maybe. But I still think Coach Donaldson will be fair. I think he already knows he's doing the wrong thing."

Stephanie laughed. "If he really wanted to be fair, he wouldn't let *me* play at all. I'm a mess. I never should have let you talk me into going out for basketball."

"You're just learning, Steph. But you've already improved a lot."

"Yeah, well, I could be twice as good and still be lousy. When I get the ball, I try to get rid of it—*fast.*"

"Hey, that's what the coach always tells us: Make quick passes."

Both girls laughed. But Jackie still wasn't in a very happy mood. She was trying to make up her mind about something. She had a plan in mind, but she didn't know whether she dared carry it out.

She decided not to mention it even to Stephanie.

At practice, on Monday, the coach gave his usual speech. He chewed on Miles for trying to take over the offense.

"Coach, I was trying to help out," Miles said. "Tommy was having trouble getting the ball up the floor with Zach all over him."

"Yeah, Coach," Tommy said. "Tip saved me—a lot of times. I couldn't get by that guy."

"Ramirez, that's just the kind of talk I don't want to hear. If you don't believe in yourself, of course you'll have trouble."

Tommy sort of shrugged. No one else dared say anything. So the first-team offense worked out against the second team. And Tommy was still with the starters.

After practice, Jackie walked out of the gym with Stephanie. She had only gone a little way when she heard Miles yell to her, "Hey, wait up."

Jackie looked back. Tip was with Kenny and Harlan. She waited for them to catch up.

"Jackie, everyone wants you to play point guard," Miles said. "With a bye this week, we'd have two weeks to practice with you in the starting lineup. And with you running the plays, I don't think anyone in the league could beat us."

Jackie shrugged. "It's not our decision," she said. "The coach has to decide."

"Not if we tell him we won't play unless he makes the change."

"Tip, that's not right," Jackie said. "Tommy would feel bad if you guys did something like that."

"He's all for it," Harlan said. "The coach has him so nervous, he feels like quitting."

"But the coach won't back down if you try to tell him what to do," Jackie said. "He'll just get all the more stubborn."

"Then we'll all quit," Miles said. "It's stupid to play if he won't put the best players on the floor."

"No. Come on. We don't want to do that."

"Well, we've got to do *something*."

"Let me do it then."

"Do what?"

"Just let me take care of it. Let me try something, and if it doesn't work, we'll talk some more. Okay?"

"Well, okay," Miles said. "But do it quick."

"I will," Jackie said.

But now she knew that she had to get her courage up. She had to face the coach, and that wouldn't be easy.

★ 6 ★

Challenge

For two days Jackie practiced a little speech—over and over. But when she stood in front of the coach, she was scared. She wasn't sure she could say the words.

"Could I talk to you for a minute?" she asked him. Her voice almost quit on her.

The coach nodded. But his face was like a rock wall.

"My big brother plays in the band at the high school," Jackie said.

The coach's eyes narrowed, as if to say, "Yeah. So what?"

His stare frightened Jackie. She forgot, for a moment, what she was going to say next. So her words came out jumbled.

"If someone wants to be first chair. Like

for trumpet. And they're second chair. Or like third, and they want to be second. Anything like that. They can challenge."

His eyes narrowed a little more.

"They ask the band teacher. Then they play something. The teacher decides who gets to be first chair—or second, or whatever."

He nodded. And he must have known what she was getting at. But he waited for her to say it.

"I just thought that might be fair for us, too. It seems like I'm as good as Tommy. And maybe I could challenge him like that. To see who gets to be the starter."

"And how are we supposed to do that?"

"I could run the offense. Then Tommy could. And maybe Miles could guard us, or something like that. And you could decide who does better."

He was staring at her again. But he didn't answer.

"It just seems like a fair way to do it," she said again.

The coach was silent for a long time. Finally he said, "Willis, I don't think girls should play against boys. I fought against having a mixed league, but I lost. So I had to take you and Stephanie on the team. But I don't like it."

This was not at all what Jackie had expected. And for the first time she felt some anger. "But we *are* on the team. And since we are, we ought to have the same chance as anyone else."

"Look, I'm the coach. I make the decisions. And I've made mine."

"You can still make the decision. I'm just asking for a chance to prove what I can do."

"I've seen what you can do, Willis. You do very well. You'll be a good player on the girls' teams in junior high."

Now Jackie really was mad. "You don't want me to prove you're wrong—in front of everyone. You're *afraid* to give me a chance."

"That's not it."

"You're scared to admit that a girl can play as well as the boys."

"Hey, you can play with them now. But the boys will get bigger and quicker. By the time you get to high school, you won't have a chance."

Jackie didn't know whether that was true

or not. But she knew there was something wrong with the man's thinking. "But I *am* playing against them now. So be fair."

Coach Donaldson's face was glowing red. "I have to think about the future, young lady. Tommy needs some confidence. How's he going to feel if he gets beat out by a *girl?*"

Jackie was stunned.

She tried to think what to say, but she couldn't.

"How can I put a girl on the floor as my point guard? My team leader? That makes every boy on the team look bad."

So that was it. Stephanie had been right—exactly right. And yet, Jackie could still hardly believe he would come right out and say it.

Even so, Jackie suddenly knew that she had won. As soon as the words were out, the coach seemed to realize that he had said the wrong thing.

"Coach, Tommy's confidence is already shot. He's playing worse all the time. You're asking him to do stuff he can't do."

"He can do it. He just needs to get his head on straight."

But something had changed. The coach's

voice had lost all its strength. He seemed embarrassed.

"The whole team knows you're not being fair. They don't care whether I'm a boy or a girl. They just want to win."

"Do you think I don't?"

"You must not. You know I play better than Tommy. And all I'm asking now is for a chance to challenge him."

"All right. Fine. We'll do just that."

And now Jackie knew that she had won for sure. The coach didn't believe for a minute that Tommy could beat her out. He had already admitted that.

Still, when he called the kids together before practice, he announced, "Jackie Willis had done a good job. So I'm giving her a chance with the first team today. Tommy will run the team part of the time, too. Then I'll decide who will start the next game."

Jackie saw how pleased everyone looked. That made her feel good. And yet, when the moment of truth came, she was nervous.

She had talked big, and now she had to prove she was right.

The coach followed her suggestion. He let

Miles guard her. And Miles came at her hard. She had to dribble under control, and she had to spot open players with Miles in her face.

At first she was a little too careful. But she soon realized she couldn't hold back.

Things started to happen.

She passed to Harlan and then cut past him. Miles stayed with her and fought his way past Harlan.

Harlan couldn't complete the give-and-go, so he passed back to Derek.

Suddenly, Jackie burst away from Miles, toward Derek. Derek passed the ball to her on the side of the lane.

Miles caught up quickly and was on her tight.

Jackie faked to her left and then turned right. She bounced a pass to Josh, who was open in the corner.

Josh took the shot, but it was off the mark. Jackie saw that it was going to hit off the front of the rim.

She darted inside Miles and was there for the rebound.

She faked Miles in the air, and then went up for a little jumper.

Swish.

Now she felt good. She had spotted the open shooter. She had used her quickness to get the rebound away from the taller players. And she had even outsmarted Tip.

"Come on, Harris," the coach shouted. "Stay on your feet until you *know* she's going up for the shot."

He sounded sort of frustrated.

Jackie liked that. She got the ball, took it out to the half-court line, and started another play. This time she tried something new.

She brought the ball toward Miles, walking slowly. She passed off to Derek, and then she tried to break down the lane for a pass back from Derek.

But Miles cut her off, and Derek couldn't get the ball to her.

He passed to Ben Riddle, who was playing in Miles's usual spot on the offense.

Ben was soon in big trouble, with Stephanie guarding him close. He dribbled a couple of times, and stopped. Now he had to pass, but he couldn't find anyone.

Jackie ran to Ben and cut around him. He handed her the ball.

She was way outside now. She had to start something new.

She used Ben for a screen, dribbled past him, and got a step on Miles. But Miles caught up quickly.

As Jackie headed for the basket, she saw Harlan cutting down the lane.

She went up for the lay-up, but Miles's hand was in the air, ready to block the shot. So Jackie shoveled the ball underhand to Harlan, who was now under the basket.

He laid the ball in for two points.

"Cut out the freelancing, Willis," the coach yelled. "Let's see you run our offense."

And so this time Jackie held up two fingers, like horns. She rushed forward, forcing Miles back enough for her to make a looping pass to Harlan on the high post.

Derek was supposed to take a pass from Harlan as he cut through the top of the key. Then Josh would set a screen for Derek.

Brett Sanders knew the play, so he tried to cut Josh off. But Josh saw that, and he used another option. He rolled away from Brett and got open on the side of the key.

Derek got the pass, but he had nowhere to go. He lobbed the ball back to Jackie. She fired a swift pass to Josh, who turned and put up the jumper.

The shot didn't go down, but the point

was made. Jackie had seen the open player and gotten the ball to him.

Coach Donaldson had soon seen enough. He put Tommy in the point guard spot, and Miles went after him.

Tommy just couldn't handle Miles. He got rattled, and he traveled the first time he brought the ball in. The next time he threw the ball away.

It didn't take long before the coach let Tommy off the hook. "Well, all right," he said. "We'll let Willis have her shot this next week."

"*All right!*" Derek almost shouted.

But the coach gave him a hard stare, and everyone else kept his mouth shut.

Coach Donaldson didn't congratulate Jackie either. In fact, he cut out half the team's drills and ended practice early.

But as soon as practice was over, the first person to congratulate Jackie was Tommy Ramirez. And after that, everyone else did too.

"We're going to win it all," Miles told Jackie. "*No one* is gonna stop us now."

And Derek pounded her back so hard, she thought she might not recover in time to play.

★ 7 ★

The Jitters

On the night before the game with the Paseo Rockets, Miles came by to see Jackie.

"I just came over to wish you luck," he said. Miles was always sure of himself. But he seemed different today—maybe nervous, maybe embarrassed.

Jackie suddenly felt kind of strange herself. She was surprised Miles would come to her house. No boy had ever done that before.

Even if Jackie hadn't admitted it to Stephanie, she did think Miles was cute.

"Well, thanks," she said. "I hope I don't mess up now that I'm finally going to start."

She was standing at the door. She didn't

know quite what to do. Then her mom said, "Hi, Miles. Come on in."

Jackie hadn't known whether Tip wanted to come in or not. But he didn't hesitate, and now she was sorry she hadn't asked him in herself.

Jackie really didn't like stuff like this. She liked playing basketball with guys, but she got nervous when she had to talk to them about anything else.

"How about a soda?" Mom was asking.

"Sure," Miles said, and he nodded. But he seemed stiff.

All that basketball smoothness was gone. He didn't even walk with his usual style.

"I'm glad Jackie made the starting lineup," he told Mrs. Willis. That was nice, but Jackie thought he was just thinking of something to say—to an adult.

"So how do you like Angel Park now that you've been here awhile?" Mrs. Willis asked.

"Well, it's not as bad as I thought at first," Miles said.

Mrs. Willis laughed a little. "That's not exactly high praise," she said. She motioned for him to sit down at the kitchen table, and he did.

She set a can of soda and a glass full of ice in front of him. "No, it's okay," Miles said. "I guess I just miss my old neighborhood."

"Why?" Jackie asked.

Miles thought about that for a second or two. "I don't know exactly. It was mostly black people down there, you know—and some Latinos. I guess I felt sort of easy with that. Out here I feel . . . different."

"But you're good friends with Kenny and Harlan, aren't you?"

"Sure. And they're okay. I didn't think I'd have such good friends who aren't black."

"Well, that's good," Mrs. Willis said.

Miles sipped at his drink. "Yeah. But still, I liked the neighborhood better. Playing ball, I knew what my friends would do. Off the court, the same. I knew how to talk, where to hang out—all that stuff. Everything's *weird* to me here."

Now Miles was relaxing. He sounded more like himself.

"I know the feeling," Mrs. Willis said. "I grew up in a black neighborhood, too. It is easier in some ways. But this is one of the things we've always fought for—equal housing and integration. If some of us don't go out and take a chance, we'll never get anywhere."

"Yeah. That's what my dad says."

Jackie laughed. "Don't you believe it?" she asked.

"I guess I do. It's a nice idea. But every morning, when I walk into that school—with all those white kids—I feel like I'm on some new planet or something. I see some Latinos, but I sure don't see many black kids."

"Kids treat you okay, though, don't they?" Jackie asked.

"Sure. Everyone talks about my hoops, and all that. But they don't treat me . . . the *same*. Not really. It's like they're being careful or something. They don't relax with me—you know—like they do with their white friends."

"They do with me," Jackie said.

"You sure?"

"Not everybody, I guess. But I've been friends with Steph since kindergarten. Her dad is Arab and her mom is English. But she couldn't be a better friend if she was black."

Miles nodded. "I guess when you grow up that way, it's kind of different."

"It is," Mrs. Willis said. "You'll find some prejudice here—just like anywhere else. But most people accept me. I feel strange sometimes when I'm at PTA or something, and everyone is white. But I don't think about it as much as I used to."

"Mom has two really close friends who are white," Jackie said.

"Do you feel as easy around them as you do with black friends?" Miles asked.

"Well . . . yes. Pretty much. But it took some time."

"Yeah, well, I guess it could be like that for me—with Kenny and Harlan. But I still miss the guys I played with back in LA."

The conversation lagged. Miles took a drink of his soda. He looked a little nervous again. "Paseo has a couple of really tall guys," he finally said. "But I don't think they're very good. We should wipe 'em out with you in the lineup."

He was suddenly drinking his soda very fast. Jackie figured he wanted to get out.

She had something she had been wanting to tell him. She figured she better do it now, or he would be gone. "Tip, thanks for not going easy on me."

"What?"

"When I challenged Tommy. You played me tough, the same as you did Tommy."

"Sure. That was the deal."

"I know. But I thought you might try to make me look good."

"No way. The coach would have spotted that right off—and that would have worked against you."

It was Mrs. Willis who said what Jackie was trying to find the words to say.

"The thing is, Miles," she said, "you gave her everything you had. That showed you had confidence in her. You knew she could handle it. That made Jackie feel good."

"Yeah, it did," Jackie said. But now she was too embarrassed to look at Miles.

Miles finished off his drink.

"Well, here's the way I thought about it," he finally said. "The coach didn't want you to make it—because you're a girl. And maybe because you're black. I'm not sure about that. But I couldn't give him a single excuse not to put you in the lineup."

"And how *did* she do?" Mrs. Willis asked.

"Oh, you should have seen her, Mrs. Willis. She was *something*. She was tougher than anyone I've had to guard all season."

Jackie loved every word of this. But she couldn't get herself to look at Miles. She tried to say, "Thanks, Tip," but the words stuck in her throat.

She did glance up long enough to see that Miles had suddenly found the table *very* interesting. He was staring straight at it.

Jackie had seen the hotshot side of Miles, plenty, and she knew how hard he tried to be cool most of the time. But she liked this nice side. He seemed almost shy.

For some reason, he even *looked* better than ever.

But Jackie didn't want to think that way. It was too complicated. For right now, she just wanted to play hoops with Miles and forget any of the other stuff.

And so she was glad when Miles said he had to go. And she was relieved when he was gone. But then she thought about him most of the evening. It was weird.

When Dad came home and heard about the visit, he teased her that she had a boyfriend now. She hated that.

And sort of liked it.

That was weird, too.

But when she wasn't thinking about Miles, she was thinking basketball. She had to do the job in the morning. It was one thing to come off the bench and play well for a while.

But this was the real thing.

Maybe the Rockets weren't that great a team. They had only won one game so far. But the coach would be only too ready for an excuse to send her back on the bench.

Jackie told herself not to worry. She had done fine every time she had played. But every time she thought about the game, she could feel her heart start to pound.

Not even Miles could make that happen.

★ 8 ★

The Test

When Jackie walked on the court, she was nervous.

Really nervous.

Her palms were sweating and her stomach was doing little flips and flops.

She told herself that she would do fine. But another side of her kept saying, "This is your test. You mess up now, and the coach will never give you another chance."

Miles walked over to her. "Don't sweat it, Jackie. The Rockets aren't that good."

"I think they're getting better, though. They won last week."

"That was against the Clippers. Everybody beats them."

"Yeah, well, the Clippers gave *us* some trouble."

"No. They gave *Tommy* some trouble. They didn't give *you* any trouble at all."

Jackie smiled. That was true and she knew it. But she also knew that all that stuff was in the past. She had to do well *today*.

Jackie pointed to a tall boy who was walking onto the floor. "That's Santos," she said. "He's pretty good. So's number twenty. His name is Watrous. I saw him play last week."

"Me, too," Miles said. "He's a gunner. He throws up three-pointers all the time, but he hardly ever makes one."

Kenny had just walked up to them. "I'm guarding him," he said.

"Are you starting?" Jackie asked.

"Yeah. The coach just told me."

Miles gave Kenny a high five and said, "*All right.* Now we've got the best players on the floor. Look out!"

Jackie was glad Kenny was playing. She thought he should have been starting all along.

"I'll try to stay tight on Watrous," Kenny said.

"I wouldn't," Miles said. "I'd give him some room when he's outside. Let him gun away. We'll get the rebounds."

"Harlan could have some trouble with Santos," Kenny said. "Santos doesn't shoot very well, but he's a tough rebounder."

"Hey, what's with you guys?" Miles said. And he laughed. "This team stinks. You make them sound like a bunch of hotshots."

"Not really," Jackie said. "But they could be tougher than you think. We have to be serious about them."

"I'll be serious. I'll put some serious points on the board, too." He grinned.

This was the side of Tip that Jackie didn't like so much. All the same, she smiled, too.

But about two minutes into the game, the smiles were gone.

Santos outjumped Harlan on the tipoff, and the Rockets' point guard—a guy named Jesse McCarty—charged down the court. He looked as though he wanted to go all the way to the hoop, but Jackie cut him off.

McCarty turned and passed to Watrous.

Watrous toed the three-point line, took aim, and fired.

Jackie remembered what Miles had said. She moved to her outlet spot. She hoped Harlan would get the rebound.

Snap!

The ball hit nothing but strings.

Three points.

Jackie told herself he got lucky. She ran over and took the inbounds pass from Kenny.

The defense dropped back, and McCarty gave Jackie plenty of room to bring the ball up the court. She dribbled quickly into the front court and looked for a pass to Harlan.

But Santos was fronting Harlan, denying him the pass. Jackie knew the Rockets' coach was wise to their plays and had told Santos what to do.

She could also see the defense was a zone. The Rockets were almost daring the Lakers to shoot from outside.

Jackie wasn't quite sure what to do.

Then she saw Josh break away from Sunny Schofield, the girl who was guarding him. Schofield was a big girl, but she wasn't fast. That was something Josh could take advantage of.

Jackie hit Josh with a quick pass. Josh drove toward the basket, but the middle was packed tight.

He pulled up and looked for someone to pass to, but he was surrounded. He finally jumped up and took a shot. He was off balance, however, and the ball banged off the front of the rim.

The rebound came right to Schofield.

She passed off to McCarty, and the Lakers fell back on defense.

Jackie went after McCarty and made him work to get the ball into the forecourt.

McCarty was not a great dribbler, but he kept his body between Jackie and the ball. He passed off to Watrous.

Watrous dribbled to the three-point line, and Kenny gave him room. Watrous let fire again.

This one didn't swish.

It rattled back and forth a couple of times . . . and then dropped through.

Jackie couldn't believe it.

"You better cover him, no matter how far outside he plays!" she yelled to Kenny.

Kenny grabbed the ball and stepped out of bounds. "All right," he said, and he tossed the ball in to her.

Jackie had a better idea what to do this time. She brought the ball to the front court, and she watched to see what Santos would do. He was fronting Harlan again.

She faked a bounce pass, and then she lobbed the ball high over Santos. Harlan leaped and took the pass, but he came down off balance. By the time he got himself under control, Schofield came over and covered him.

Harlan spotted Miles cutting toward the hoop, and he hit him with a pass.

Miles went right on by Watrous. He drove straight to the hoop and laid the ball up . . . but not in.

The ball rolled over the back of the rim.

Santos grabbed the rebound, and the Rockets were back in business.

McCarty brought the ball up quickly this time. He passed off to Santos, but Harlan was on him tight.

Santos passed back to McCarty, and Jackie got all over him. She almost made the steal, but Watrous charged over to help.

McCarty got the ball to him.

Watrous turned and fired up another bomb before Kenny could cover him.

But this one was way short.

Air ball!

Jackie was relieved to see that he could miss.

But Santos jumped high to catch the shot—as though it had been a pass. Then he laid the ball in for two.

The game had hardly begun, and the score was already 8 to 0.

Jackie was worried.

She heard Coach Donaldson yell, "Willis, call time out."

She did as she was told, but she was scared that the coach had made up his mind already. Maybe she would be out of the game before her team even scored.

Jackie could feel the panic spreading through the team. They jogged over to the side of the court, by the coach, but then they all started talking at the same time.

"All right now, calm down," Coach Donaldson said. "Just listen to me."

"Willis, you had the right idea. Feed a couple of lob passes to Harlan, and their center will stop fronting him. If he doesn't, we'll beat them that way all day."

"Okay," Jackie said, and she took a deep breath. She was staying in the game. The coach had actually said that she had done the right thing.

"Sandoval, you stay on that number twenty

like he's your Siamese twin. He's their only shooter—so don't let him shoot."

"All right," Kenny said.

Jackie knew that Kenny could do it, too.

"And here's the other thing. If they want to pack in, let's show them who can shoot from outside. We've got a lot better shooters than they do."

That was the most positive thing Coach Donaldson had said all season. It sounded good.

It also happened to be the very thing that Miles had told him—the very thing, in fact, that had made him mad.

Had the coach actually listened—no matter what he had said?

The kids went back on the floor.

Jackie looked for Harlan. He was still fronted, but the forwards were playing in tight. Jackie was afraid to lob the ball into a crowd.

She passed to Kenny, who looked for Miles. He was open outside, and Kenny got the ball to him.

Miles popped a jumper—smooth as silk.
Two!

The Lakers were on the board.

Jackie tried to steal the inbounds pass. She missed the steal, but she made things tough for McCarty.

He tried to angle across the court and not take Jackie on directly. And then, when she stayed tough, he passed off to Watrous. But Kenny covered him tight.

He dribbled a couple of times and stopped because he was about to lose the ball. McCarty ran over to help, but just as he got the pass, the whistle blew.

"Ten seconds," the ref shouted. "Ball goes over to the red team."

Great! They hadn't made it across the midcourt line in ten seconds. She and Kenny had made things too tough for them.

Jackie got the sideline pass and headed for the forecourt. She watched McCarty fall back.

So she dribbled straight to the three-point line and took the shot herself.

Pop! Three points.

The Lakers had some outside shooters of their own. And now the team was right back in the game, 8 to 5.

Jackie felt her confidence come back. She could do the job!

★ 9 ★

Fire the Rockets

Things were looking up for the Lakers.

Miles hit a couple more outside shots, and Josh banged another one in. That began to spread the zone as the forwards came out to cover Miles and Josh.

Once that happened, Jackie was able to lob the ball to Harlan. He picked up an easy basket.

On defense, Kenny made life almost impossible for Watrous. The guy was lucky to get the ball, let alone get a shot off.

The other players didn't shoot well. Only Santos, with his height and strength, was keeping the Rockets in the game. He kept grabbing offensive rebounds and putting them in.

Early in the second quarter, the score was 19 to 14 for the Lakers.

But the Rockets weren't ready to give up. They didn't have as much talent as some teams, but they were well coached.

This time it was the Rockets who called time out.

Their coach had them switch to a high-pressure man-to-man defense and a full-court press.

Now Jackie had to work to get the ball up the floor.

But work she did.

And she made it look easy.

She was a good dribbler, but even more, she could spot the players who were open at the other end of the court. Twice she lofted long passes that resulted in easy baskets for the Lakers.

The Rockets soon had to fall back and forget their press.

Jackie then began to take advantage of the man-to-man in the forecourt. She made good passes and ran the offense well.

It could have been an easy game.

But it wasn't.

Maybe Miles had never taken the Rockets seriously. Or maybe he was just having an off day. For some reason, he wasn't hitting his shots the way he usually did.

In fact, the shots weren't dropping that well for any of the Lakers.

The Rockets' offense had turned into a one-man show. Kenny had taken Watrous right out of the game, but Santos was going crazy.

Poor Harlan just couldn't cover the guy.

Santos was stronger and more experienced. He was making most of his shots off rebounds or off deep feeds under the basket. Harlan couldn't seem to do anything about it.

At halftime the coach got all over Harlan. The score was 27 to 21, but the Lakers just couldn't open up a big lead.

"You're just standing there!" Coach Donaldson told Harlan. "You're letting him slip away from you. You don't block out."

"I try, but he always—"

"Don't give me excuses, Sloan. Just go out

there and do the job. Or I'll find someone who can."

Harlan tried.

But he didn't do any better. As the second half got going, Santos scored four quick points. The coach sent Brett Sanders in the game for Harlan.

But he was definitely worse.

So the coach chewed on Harlan some more and sent him back.

The only trouble was, some of the other players hadn't had a chance to play yet. When the coach sent Derek in for Kenny, Watrous started launching the long shots again.

As it turned out, Miles was right. Watrous didn't hit that many.

And Harlan was fighting harder.

But Santos was still picking up too many offensive rebounds.

And so the score stayed close.

The coach soon sent Kenny back in, but he gave Tommy a chance to play point guard.

That didn't go well either. After about three minutes, the coach sent Jackie back.

The Lakers got the lead up to ten a couple of times, but then it would drop back to six, once even four.

The Lakers just couldn't put them away.

And then, halfway through the fourth quarter, the Rockets made a run.

Watrous hit a three-pointer—with Kenny all over him. And then McCarty let fly with another one.

And that one also went in!

The lead was back to four, 48 to 44.

Miles came back with a rebound and a fall-away jumper for two. He was getting serious now.

But Schofield matched him with a bucket of her own—only her second one all day.

And then everyone went cold.

No one hit a basket on either side, and Harlan even missed *two* foul shots.

Time was getting short, and the Lakers' lead was still at four.

Then Santos muscled past Harlan for a lay-up, and the lead was down to two.

Jackie knew her team *had* to get a hoop this time down the floor. Their momentum was in the drain.

And so she called for a clear-out and got the ball to Tip. He was the guy to go to in a situation like this—even on a bad day.

Miles made a good move, but Watrous stayed with him.

Jackie saw what was happening, and she cut toward the basket.

She beat McCarty and took a good pass from Miles. But as she got to the hoop, McCarty reached over her head and slammed the ball away.

Her breath caught for a moment until she heard the whistle.

Fouled in the act of shooting.

Two shots.

Jackie walked to the foul line. She felt good. She liked having control of the situation when the pressure was on.

"You just fouled the wrong player," Miles told McCarty. "She'll make 'em."

Jackie liked that.

She looked at the clock. Just under a minute to play. She could get the lead back to four. But if she missed the shots, the Rockets would have a chance to tie.

No way. She just couldn't let that happen.

The referee tossed her the ball, and she bounced it a couple of times. "Relax," she told herself, out loud. "Smooth and easy—and follow through." She took a steady bead on the front of the rim and held her breath as she cocked the ball high.

And then she released the shot.

Swish!

She breathed again. For the first time all day, Jackie noticed the crowd. She heard her mom yelling, "Do it again, honey. No problem."

"That's right. No problem," Jackie told herself, but when the ref bounced the ball back to her, her breath caught again.

She dribbled the ball twice again, brought the ball up exactly the same way—released with that same flowing motion.

And . . . *Swish!*

The Rockets grabbed the ball and tried to get something going, but they looked frantic. Watrous tried another one of his bombs, and it was way off.

The ball bounced off the glass, and Josh got in for the rebound.

Josh tossed the ball to Jackie, and McCarty fouled her.

Now Jackie's confidence was flying high. She canned two more foul shots, and that was it.

The Lakers won, 54 to 48.

Jackie got mobbed.

Everyone on the team—and all the parents—took turns slapping her back.

She took some real battering—especially from Derek—but she loved every minute of it.

"You're *good*, Jackie. You're *good*," Tip told her. Jackie liked that a lot. Miles didn't usually like to admit that anyone outside LA could play the game.

But the big surprise was Coach Donaldson.

He waited until everyone else had taken a turn, and then he stepped in front of her. The front of him seemed to be a whole acre of gray cotton. And he didn't show the slightest sign that he was happy.

For a moment, from the look on his face, Jackie thought he was going to chew her out.

But what he said almost knocked Jackie down. "I was wrong," he said, rather softly. "I knew you could play, but I didn't want to admit it to myself. I'm old fashioned. I've just always thought that girls ought to play with dolls and not get out there and bang around with the boys."

Jackie had no idea what to say. "I just . . . wanted a chance," she finally mumbled.

"Well, you deserved it. This team, more than anything else, has needed a leader. And now it has one."

Jackie nodded. "Thanks," she said.

"Now you're going to have to work harder than ever," he said. "I'm going to make you into a great ball player."

But somewhere, just toward the end of his sentence, he smiled—ever so little.

Jackie knew that now she had seen everything!

League Standings After Seven Games

Angel Park Bulls	5–1
Santa Rita Jazz	5–1
Angel Park Lakers	4–2
Blue Springs Warriors	4–2
Paseo Rockets	2–4
San Lorenzo Suns	1–5
Cactus Hills Clippers	0–6

Fourth Game Scores:

Angel Park Lakers	54	San Lorenzo Suns	45
Blue Springs Warriors	43	Paseo Rockets	31
Santa Rita Jazz	49	Angel Park Bulls	46
Cactus Hills Clippers	bye		

Fifth Game Scores:

Angel Park Lakers	55	Cactus Hills Clippers	42
Angel Park Bulls	61	Paseo Rockets	29
Blue Springs Warriors	52	San Lorenzo Suns	28
Santa Rita Jazz	bye		

Sixth Game Scores:

Santa Rita Jazz	46	San Lorenzo Suns	39
Paseo Rockets	34	Cactus Hills Clippers	32
Angel Park Bulls	50	Blue Springs Warriors	46
Angel Park Lakers	bye		

Seventh Game Scores:

Angel Park Lakers	54	Paseo Rockets	48
Santa Rita Jazz	58	Blue Springs Warriors	52
Angel Park Bulls	63	Cactus Hills Clippers	19
San Lorenzo Suns	bye		

Angel Park Hoop Stars Strategies

The Zone

An offense is only as good as its defense. The key to a successful defense is how well it can **read** and react to the offensive strengths and weaknesses of an opponent. A familiar defense is the **man-to-man**. However, when defending against an opponent with poor outside shooting or one dominated by a high-scoring player, a **zone** defense can be effective.

By fanning out defenders around the key area, the zone defense attempts to limit ofensive penetration into the lane. Zone defenses are 1-2-2, 2-1-2, 1-3-1, or 2-3. Typically, the center is positioned **underneath** in the paint, flanked on either side by the forwards and fronted by the two guards. Defenders shift right or left with the movement of the ball.

A zone is not foolproof. A zone can be **broken**. Outside, or **perimeter**, shooting will lure a defender away from her position, exposing a gap, or **seam**, in the lane. Likewise, crisp passing and lots of running and cutting can catch sleepy zone defenders off guard.

1-2-2

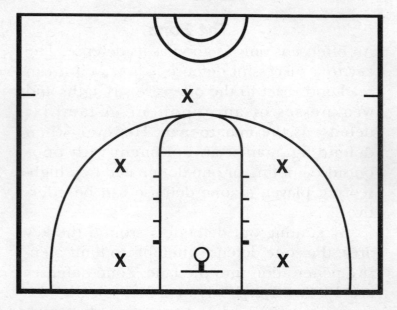

The **1-2-2** is the most popular zone defense because it minimizes the weaknesses of other zones. Yet players in the **1-2-2** must be careful to coordinate how they will cover offensive players "in the paint"; otherwise they will be vulnerable to inside scoring.

2-1-2

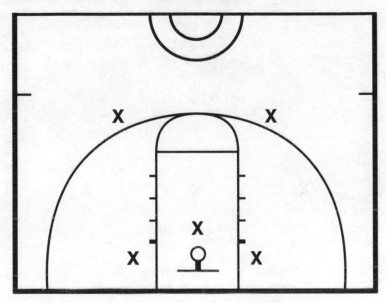

The **2-1-2** zone allows good shooting from the corners and the foul line area, but it shuts down drives to the basket from the corners and the wings.

1-3-1

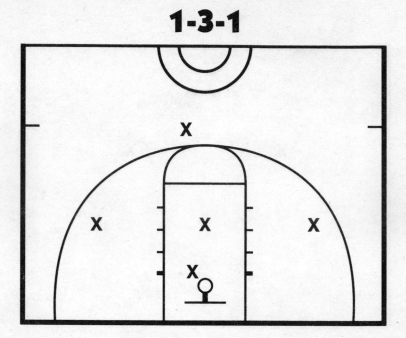

The **1-3-1** zone leaves the corners exposed to drives or cuts to the basket but stops jump shots from the upper post and defends well against passing from the wings.

2-3

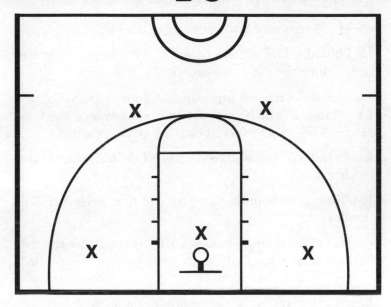

A **2-3** zone allows good passing from the wings and leaves the foul line area more open for shooting but can be very effective stopping shooting – and drives to the basket – from the corners.

Glossary

airball An embarrassing shot that falls far short of the basket.

assist A pass that leads directly to a score.

backboard The rectangular or semicircular surface onto which the rim is mounted.

backcourt The area from the baseline to the midcourt line through which the offense must advance the ball after a score. Also refers to the two guard positions.

bank shot A shot that rebounds off the backboard into the hoop.

baseline The boundary line, or end line, at each end of the floor.

basket The 18-inch-diameter ring through which the ball must pass for a player to score points. Also called "hoop," "rim," or "iron."

bench The nonstarting members of a team.

block To repel a shot at any point on its upward arc. Also called "reject."

box out To square the body toward the basket in an effort to screen an opponent from getting a rebound. Also called "block out."

brick A low-arc shot that bangs clumsily off the rim. Taking terrible shots is called "throwing up bricks."

center The middle position in a three-player front line, usually the tallest member of the team.

charge A foul on a ball handler for running into a stationary defensive player who has established position.

clear out To free, or isolate, a ball handler to go one-on-one with a defender by rotating offensive players to the opposite side of the floor.

crash the boards To hustle for rebounds coming off the backboard.

cut A quick move by a player without the ball toward the basket for a possible pass.

double dribble An infraction in which a ball handler dribbles with both hands simultaneously or resumes a dribble after having stopped.

double-team Two players defending one opponent, also called "trapping."

downtown A shot taken far away from the basket.

drive To dribble hard toward the basket for a close shot at the goal.

fake Any move by a ball handler to deceive a defender into an off balance position, such as a "head fake" or "pump fake."

fast break A hustling transition offense in which players move quickly upcourt before opponents can fall back on defense.

forward Either of the two outside positions in a three-player front line.

foul Illegal contact or unsportsmanlike conduct that may result in either a change of possession or a free throw for the player fouled.

free throw An undefended shot at the basket from a distance of 15 feet from the end line, awarded to a player who has been fouled.

free throw lane The 12-foot-wide rectangular area inside the free throw lines. Also called the "lane," "underneath," or the "paint."

give and go A maneuver in which a player passes to a teammate, cuts to the basket, and looks for a quick return pass.

guard Either of the two backcourt positions. A point guard usually calls plays and brings the ball upcourt; the off guard is often the team's best shooter.

hail mary A desperation shot at the basket.

held ball When opposing players have equal possession of the ball, resulting in a "jump ball." Instead of jumping, however, most teams today alternate possession as indicated by the possession arrow.

inbound To bring the ball into play after a score, turnover, or other stoppage of play.

jump ball The play that begins the game wherein a ball is tossed into the air above and between two opposing players by the referee.

key The area that includes the free throw lane and free throw circle.

man-to-man defense A method of defense in which each member of the defensive team is designated to guard a particular member of the offensive team.

midcourt line The boundary that divides the playing surface into two equal halves, also called the "ten-second line."

outlet pass A transition pass from a rebounder to a teammate usually positioned at or near either sideline.

pivot The act of keeping one foot in place while holding the ball and moving the other foot one step in any direction.

point   A position in the front court, usually at the top of the key. A point guard might "pull up" here to signal a play.

post   The position the center plays on offense. In a "high post," the center plays near the top of the free throw circle. In a "low post," the center plays near the basket.

press   An aggressive type of defense in which players guard opponents very closely, designed to induce an opponent into committing a turnover.

rainbow   A pretty outside shot with a very high arc, as opposed to an airball.

screen   An offensive play in which a teammate, by establishing position, blocks a defender from guarding the ball handler, leaving him open for an uncontested shot. Also called a "pick."

shot   An aimed throw of the ball at the hoop. Familiar shots are the "jump shot," the "lay-up," the "hook shot," the "slam dunk," the "fadeaway jumper," and the "three-point shot."

showtime   Fast-paced and flashy style of play.

switch   A maneuver in which two teammates on defense shift assignments so that each guards the opponent usually guarded by the other.

ten seconds   The amount of time an offensive team has to inbound the ball from the baseline past the midcourt—or "ten-second"—line. A violation results in change of possession.

three-seconds violation   An infraction in which an offensive player remains inside the free throw lane for more than the permitted three seconds at a time.

tip-in   A field goal made when a player taps the ball in after a missed field goal attempt.

trailer   A player who follows closely, or "trails," a ball handler driving to the basket, either to rebound or to receive a quick pass for a basket.

transition   The act of switching from defense to offense, and vice versa.

travel   An infraction in which a ball handler takes more than two steps without dribbling or passing, resulting in a turnover. Also called "walk."

turnover   The loss of possession of the ball to the opposing team, through mistakes or infractions of the rules.

wings   The areas just below the free throw line and to the sides of the lane. Often the best point to begin an offensive attack.

zone defense   A method of defense in which each member of the defensive team guards a specified portion, or "zone," of the playing area.

Play ball with the kids from Angel Park!

ANGEL PARK ALL-STARS™

by Dean Hughes

Meet Kenny, Harlan, and Jacob—three talented young rookies on Angel Park's Little League team. They're in for plenty of hard-hitting fastball action...as well as fun and friendship. You'll want to read them all!

#1 **Making the Team**

#2 **Big Base Hit**

#3 **Winning Streak**

#4 **What a Catch!**

#5 **Rookie Star**

#6 **Pressure Play**

#7 **Line Drive**

#8 **Championship Game**

#9 **Superstar Team**

#10 **Stroke of Luck**

#11 **Safe at First**

#12 **Up to Bat**

#13 **Play-off**

#14 **All Together Now**

BULLSEYE BOOKS PUBLISHED BY ALFRED A. KNOPF, INC.

The all-star soccer action starts here!

ANGEL PARK
SOCCER STARS™

by Dean Hughes

Jacob Scott is back with some new friends and a whole
new sport—soccer. Join the Angel Park Pride as they
pass, shoot, and score their way toward the league
championship. Filled with the same nonstop action as
the Angel Park All-Stars, you'll want them all for your
collection!

#1 **Kickoff Time**   #4 **Psyched!**

#2 **Defense!**   #5 **Backup Goalie**

#3 **Victory Goal**   #6 **Total Soccer**

BULLSEYE BOOKS PUBLISHED BY ALFRED A. KNOPF, INC.